Nathan and Father
A WALK OF WONDER

written and illustrated by
KIM G. OVERTON

FLYING WREN STUDIO
Petoskey, MI

Published by Flying Wren Studio, Petoskey, MI

Publisher's Cataloging-in-Publication Data
Overton, Kim G.

Nathan and father : a walk of wonder / written and illustrated by Kim G. Overton. – Petoskey, MI : Flying Wren Studio, 2017.

p. ; cm.

ISBN13: 978-0-9980141-0-4

1. Father and child—Juvenile fiction. I. Title.

PZ7.5.O84 2017
[E]–dc23   2017931731

Project coordination by Jenkins Group, Inc.
www.BookPublishing.com

Design by Yvonne Fetig Roehler

Printed in Malaysia by Tien Wah Press (PTE) Limited, First Printing, February 2017
21 20 19 18 17 · 5 4 3 2 1

For Stacy, Drew, Meg, Stephanie, and Eric,
whom I had not yet met when I wrote this,
and who now answer my questions.

For Nolan, Christopher, Elijah, Connor, and George...because you are.

For Brian, Ian, and Zach, for your journey.
Thank you for being that father.

For children all around this world of wonder
who ask good questions
and for the adults who answer with love.

This West African Adinkra symbol represents the power of love.

Its English translation is "Love never loses its way home."

Nathan and Father went walking one day;
Nathan and Father went walking.

They saw many things,
and Nathan saw more,
and so he could not keep from talking.

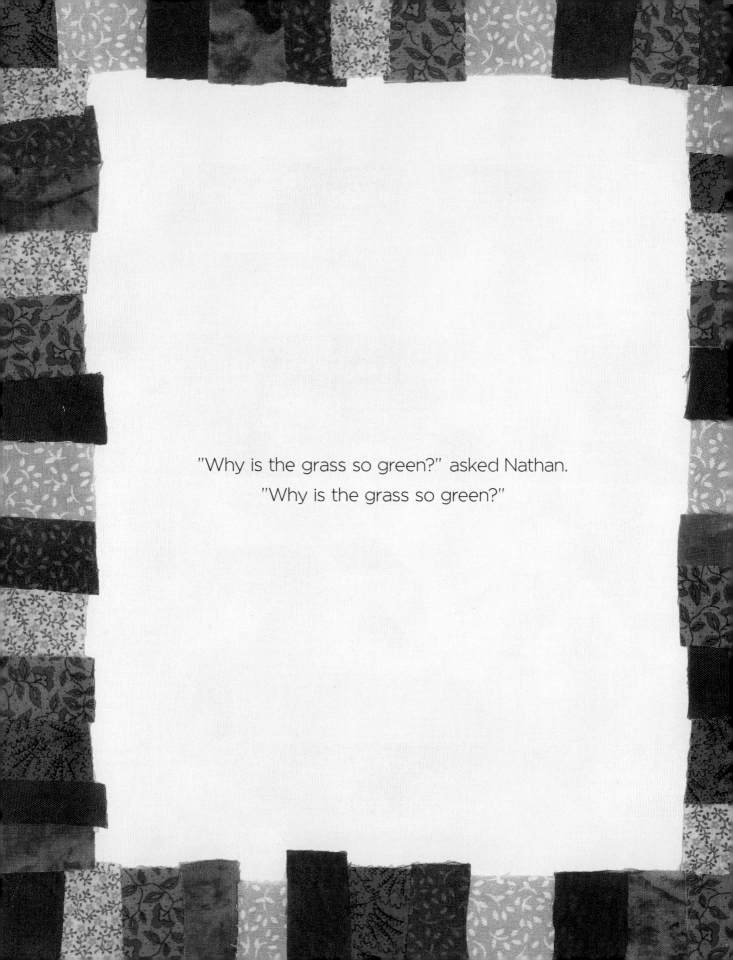

"Why is the grass so green?" asked Nathan.
"Why is the grass so green?"

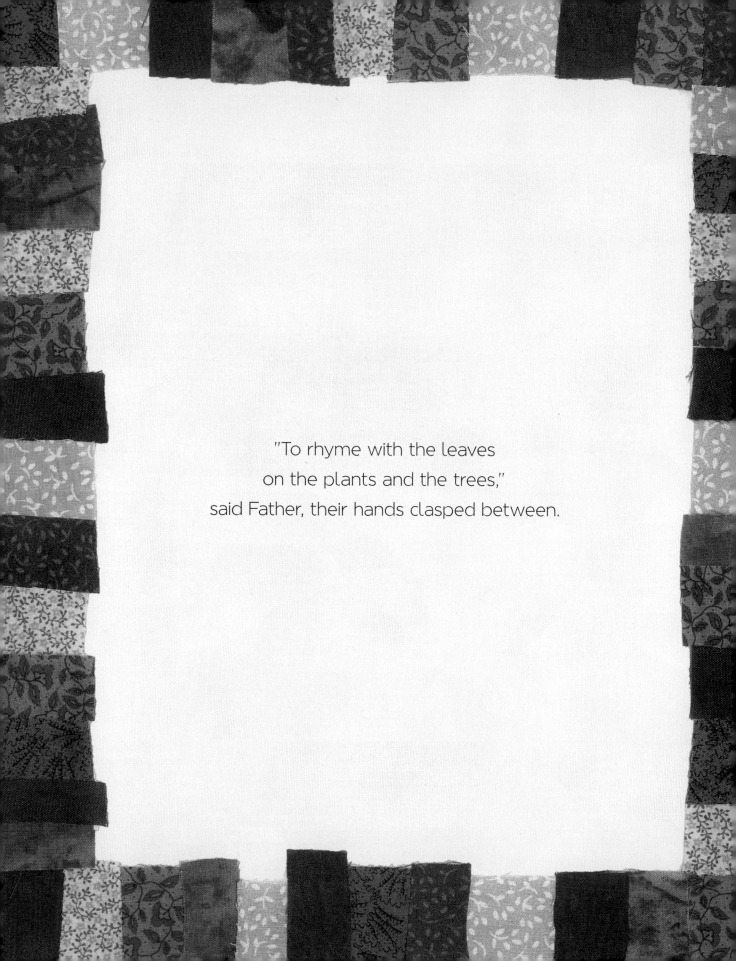

"To rhyme with the leaves
on the plants and the trees,"
said Father, their hands clasped between.

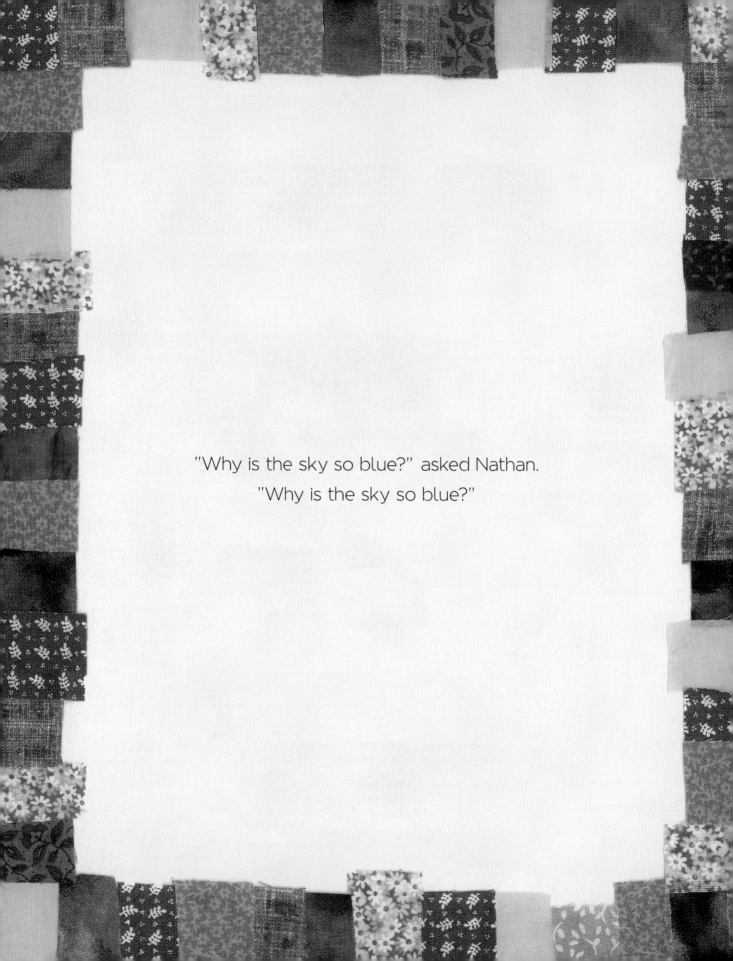

"Why is the sky so blue?" asked Nathan.
"Why is the sky so blue?"

"It matches the sparkles of blue
in your eyes,"
said Father, and on walked the two.

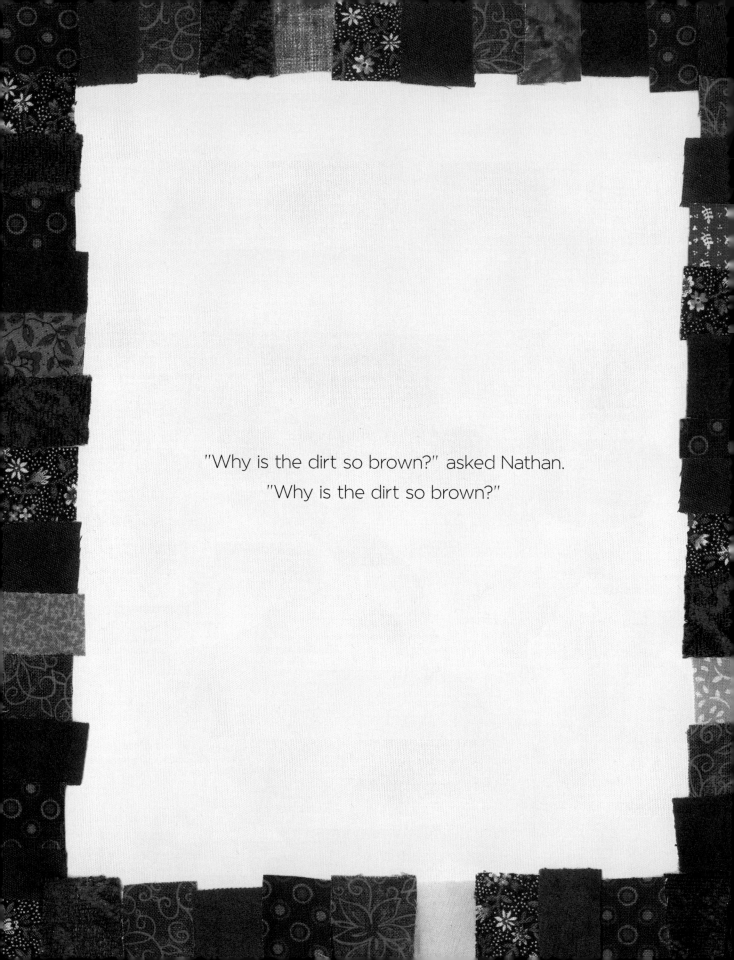

"Why is the dirt so brown?" asked Nathan.
"Why is the dirt so brown?"

"The ants and the snakes
seem to like it that way,"
said Father, looking thoughtfully down.

"Why is the sun so gold?" asked Nathan.

"Why is the sun so gold?"

"Because it's so bright,
we can see with its light,"
said Father, his eyes kind and bold.

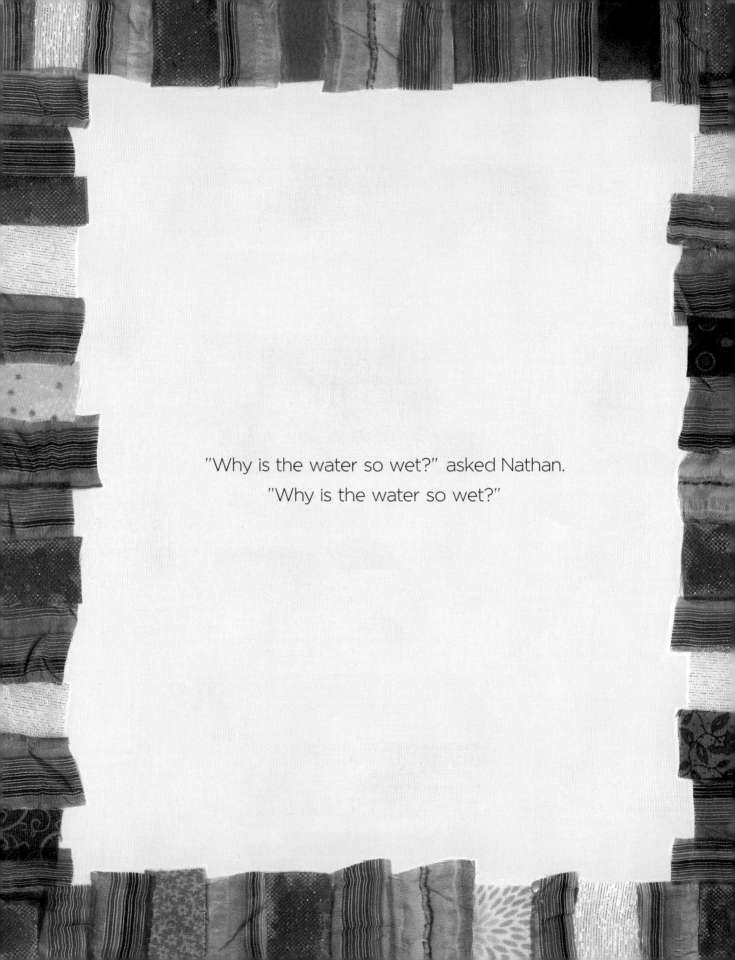

"Why is the water so wet?" asked Nathan.
"Why is the water so wet?"

"Because, in the desert,
the sand is so dry,"
said Father, and they watched the sun set.

"Who hung the stars up so high?" asked Nathan.

"Who hung the stars up so high?"

"Whoever made snow
on the mountaintops glow,"
said Father, surveying the sky.

"Why do you love me?" asked Nathan with wonder.
"Why do you love me?" asked Nathan.

And Nathan's eyes drooped
as he hugged Father's neck.
"Because you are Nathan," said Father.

Kim G. Overton

Kim Overton's art career began in the seventh grade, when someone purchased her purple papier-mâché hippopotamus wearing white lace-up sneakers. In the intervening years, she has opened a bookstore, coached gymnastics, raised five pretty wonderful children, co-founded an arts-integrated K–12 school, taught math and art, served as elementary principal for the International School of Ouagadougou in West Africa, and taught homeschooled families.

Kim lives near the shores of Lake Michigan, making art that celebrates the magnificence of nature. She would love to hear from you at kim@flyingwrenstudio.com.

Also illustrated by Kim Overton

Sip, Pick, and Pack...How Pollinators Help Plants Make Seeds
by Polly Cheney, published by Orange Frazer Press.